Hooray for Marcia Wernick!

Balzer + Bray is an imprint of HarperCollins Publishers.

Hooray for Amanda & Her Alligator!

www.harpercollinschildrens.com

Library of Congress Cataloging-in-Publication Data
Willems, Mo.
 Hooray for Amanda & her alligator! / written and illustrated by Mo Willems.—1st ed.
  p. cm.
 Summary: Amanda and her alligator have lots of fun together, but when
Amanda's grandfather buys her a panda, Alligator must learn to make new friends.
 ISBN 978-0-06-200400-0
 [1. Friendship—Fiction. 2. Alligators—Fiction. 3. Toys—Fiction.] I. Title.
PZ7.W65535Am 2011   2010009633
[E]—dc22   CIP
                                                      AC

Typography by Martha Rago
11 12 13 14 15 LPR 10 9 8 7 6 5 4 3 2
❖
First Edition

HOORAY FOR Amanda & Her Alligator!

words and pictures by
Mo Willems

BALZER + BRAY   *An Imprint of* HarperCollins*Publishers*

· 1 ·
A Surprising Surprise

Table of Contents

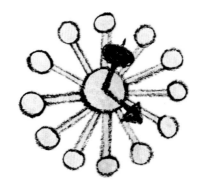

Amanda was at the library
getting her books for the week.

Her alligator was not.

He was waiting for Amanda
to get back.

I do not like it when Amanda is gone, thought Alligator.
I am no good at waiting.

He paced around the room.

He fiddled with his tail.

When Amanda comes home, we will have fun, thought Alligator.

Maybe she will have a surprise for me!

Alligator smiled.

Finally, Amanda came back to her room.

"Do you have a surprise for me?" asked Alligator.

"Do you want a surprise?" asked Amanda.

He did.

"BOO!" yelled Amanda.

"EEK!" yelled Alligator.

"You always bring home the most interesting surprises,"
said Alligator.

· 2 ·

An Un-Surprising Surprise

Amanda was reading her new library book *How to Raise a Tiger* when her alligator snuck into the room.

He giggled.

"I have a surprise for you," said Alligator. "Would you like it?"

He giggled some more.

"Is it you yelling 'BOO!'?" asked Amanda.

"Uh," said Alligator, "not anymore."

"You'd better put on your Old Thinking Cap if you want
to surprise me!" Amanda said as her alligator left the room.

And that . . .

is just what Alligator did.

· 2½ ·
An Extra Surprise

Alligator still had a perfectly good, unused "BOO!"
and no one to give it to.

So he gave it to himself.

· 3 ·

A Surprising Tickle

Amanda was reading her new library book *Whale Songs for Beginners* when her alligator came into the room.

He was wearing his
Old Thinking Cap.

"Something tickles," said Alligator.

"What tickles?" asked Amanda.

"I DO!" yelled Alligator.

And he did.

(Good Old Thinking Cap.)

· 4 ·
A Surprising Value

Amanda was reading her new library book
Climbing Things for Fun and Profit when
her alligator came into the room.

He was not wearing his Thinking Cap
when he said, "Something tickles."

"That was a funny joke," said Amanda.
"But I'm not going to fall for it again."

"No, really," said Alligator.

(When friends say "No, really," they mean it.)

Amanda helped her alligator find what tickled.
Something was attached to his tail.

"It's a price tag," said Amanda.

"Read it! Read it!"
said Alligator.

"I have always wanted to know how much I am worth!"

Amanda read the tag.

"It says seven cents."

"Seven cents!" gasped Alligator.
"Why am I only worth seven cents!?"

Amanda did not say anything.

"Tell the truth!" said Alligator.

(When friends ask you to tell the truth,
you tell the truth.)

"You were in the sale bucket," said Amanda.

"I was in the sale bucket!" said Alligator.
"Why was I in the sale bucket?"

(Amanda told her alligator the truth.)

"No one wanted to buy you," she said.

"I am afraid to ask, but I must know," said Alligator.

"Why did no one want to buy me?"

Amanda told her alligator, "No one wanted to buy you because they knew you were meant to be my best friend."

After that, Alligator felt better.

(And that's the truth.)

· 5 ·
A Surprising Solution

GRUMBLE

Amanda was reading her new
library book *You Can Make It
Yourself: Jet Packs!* when
she noticed her alligator
chewing on her head.

"Stop that!" said Amanda.

"I'm bored," replied Alligator.

"I always say, 'Books beat boredom,'" said Amanda wisely.

Alligator decided to give it a try.

He went to the bookshelf.
He looked at the books.
He picked out a book.

Well, what do you know, thought Alligator. Books *do* beat boredom.

But Amanda's head tastes better.

· 6 ·

A Surprising Discovery

Amanda was at the zoo with her grandpa.

Her alligator was not.

He was waiting for Amanda to get back.

I do not like it when Amanda is gone, thought Alligator again.
I am no good at waiting.

He paced around the room again.

He fiddled with his tail again.

He tried to eat another book,
but his heart was not in it.

When Amanda comes home, we will have fun, thought Alligator.

We will sing silly songs!
We will dress up!
We will make discoveries!

Maybe Amanda will have
another surprise for me!

Alligator smiled.

"Surprise!" yelled Amanda, swinging open the door. "Look what Grandpa got for me at the zoo!"

It was a panda.

The panda was huge.

The panda was fluffy.

The panda did not look like it came from the sale bucket.

Alligator did not like Amanda's surprise.

"Nice to meet you," said the panda.

"Whatever," replied Alligator.

"Oh!" cried Amanda. "I have to go. Grandpa is taking me to dinner!"

Amanda skipped out of the room.

The panda looked around the room.
"What do we do now?" she asked.

"We wait," replied Alligator.

Alligator and the panda waited.

After a very short wait, the panda suddenly barked, "I am
no good at waiting!

I am better at singing silly songs!
Or dressing up!
Or making discoveries!"

Alligator looked at Panda.

That evening, Alligator sang a silly song.

That evening, Panda dressed up.

That evening, Alligator made a discovery.

He had a new friend.